FRIGHTVILLE

THE HAUNTED KEY

BY MIKE FORD

Scholastic Inc.

ISBN 978-1-338-36013-4

10 9 8 7 6 5 4 3 2 1 20 21 22 23 24

Printed in the U.S.A. 40
First printing 2020

Book design by Stephanie Yang

FOR VINZ

1

"Did you get it open?"

Sofia tried turning the key that she'd inserted into the lock on the trunk. It didn't budge. She twisted it again, then rattled the lock in frustration. It was the ninth key she'd tried.

"No," she said. "And that was the last one on the ring."

Her father came over and attempted to turn the key himself.

"I already *did* that," Sofia said.

"Just making sure," said Mr. Flores, pulling the key out. "Sometimes these old locks stick when they haven't been used in a while."

Sofia sat down on the trunk and let out an exasperated sigh. Then she looked around the attic. The bare wood floor was covered in dust, and the only light came from a single tiny window at the far end of the room. It was covered with dirt and cobwebs, so the attic was shrouded in shadows. Fortunately, her father had brought a flashlight, which was how they had noticed the trunk pushed into one corner of the attic.

The rest of the room was filled with cots, or at least metal frames that were supposed to have mattresses on them. Only one did. The rest were bare. There were seven on each of the two long walls of the attic.

"Why are there so many beds in here?" Sofia asked.

"People had a lot more kids back when this house was built," her father answered, poking at a hole in the ceiling where it looked like water was getting in. "One more thing to add to the to-do list," he muttered.

"But there are plenty of bedrooms downstairs," said Sofia.

In fact, there were nine bedrooms in the house. It's why her father had bought it in the first place, why they had moved from their little apartment in the city to the big old place in Sorrow's Hollow. He thought it would make a great bed-and-breakfast.

"Maybe they had boarders," her father

suggested. "That was a big thing back then, renting rooms to people who couldn't afford their own houses."

Sofia supposed this might explain it. She still thought it was odd, though. She stared hard at the trunk, as if her glare might make it feel bad for being so stubborn about opening up for her. "Why would the people we bought the house from leave a locked trunk in the attic?"

"Who knows," her father said, examining the bunch of keys in his hand and jangling them. "Maybe they forgot about it. It looks like no one has been up here in years. Or maybe there's nothing in it."

Sofia was annoyed. They had been in the house for only a few days, and she wasn't exactly excited about it. She missed their apartment in the city. She missed her friends. The locked trunk felt like one more reminder that her life had changed, and not for the better.

"Nothing works in this house," she said angrily. "There's no hot water in the bathroom. We don't get Wi-Fi. And there's no air-conditioning. It was so hot last night! I thought I was going to melt!"

"And yet, you didn't," said her father. "Look, I know this house isn't perfect. But it will be, with a little work. You'll see. It's going to be beautiful, and everyone is going to want to stay here."

Sofia snorted. "Maybe people who like creepy old houses will," she said. "Everyone else will go to places where there's actually something to do."

"Hey, there's lots to do around here," her father countered. "There's hiking, and fishing, and tubing on the creek. And next month there's the Firefly Festival."

"Fireflies," Sofia said. "Wow. I can't wait."

"I have to go to the hardware store in town," her father said, pretending not to see her rolling her eyes. "Why don't you come with me? I bet we can find a fan for your room there. And I'm pretty sure the real estate agent said there's a bookstore."

At the mention of books, Sofia perked up a little. Books were always good. She was currently reading Lucy M. Boston's *The Children of Green Knowe*, and she had only a few chapters left. Maybe she would be able to find the next book in the series in town. She followed her father out of the attic and down the stairs.

"Aren't you going to lock the front door?" she asked as he descended the front steps and walked toward the beat-up red pickup truck he'd bought to get around now that they didn't have the subway or bus.

"What for?" her father said. "This isn't the city. What could possibly happen in Sorrow's Hollow?"

"Nothing," Sofia mumbled as she walked to the truck and got in. "That's the problem."

The hardware store was out of fans, and Sofia's mood had not improved by the time they finished picking up the other things they needed. Back outside, she looked around for the bookstore her father had mentioned. None of the stores really seemed like they might carry books, but one of the nearby windows was filled with some curious things. Sofia looked at the name painted on the door.

"Frightville," she said. "Doesn't sound like a bookstore to me."

"Maybe whoever runs it knows where the bookstore is," her father suggested. "Let's go ask."

Sofia pushed the door open, and she and her father stepped inside. The store was stuffed with things. All kinds of things. Sofia didn't know where to look first. Her eyes moved from a clown marionette dangling from its strings to a large dollhouse in which a family of what appeared to be real mice was celebrating a birthday party. The store was eerie and magical all at once, like a junk shop and carnival combined, and Sofia wanted to examine everything.

Then a man appeared. Quite tall and quite thin, he wore a black suit and had silver hair and pale skin, as if he'd lived his whole life indoors and never seen the sun. "I am Odson Ends," he said in a low, smooth voice. "Welcome to my shop. May I help you find something?"

"I was actually looking for the bookstore," Sofia told him.

"I do have a number of books," the man said. He tilted his head, peering at Sofia with interest before lifting one long, bony finger and pointing it at her. "But I think you're looking for something else."

"I am?" Sofia said. "Oh, well, I couldn't find a fan at the hardware store."

"Mmm," said Mr. Ends, shaking his head. "I don't think that's it."

Sofia laughed. "Well, unless you have a key that can open a locked trunk, I can't think of anything else."

The man smiled. "A key," he said thoughtfully. "Now *that* I may be able to help you with."

He walked away, going to a cupboard and opening it. When he came back, he was holding an old wooden box. He lifted the lid, and inside were dozens of keys of all shapes and sizes. He held the box out.

"Do they all open trunks?" Sofia asked, looking at the jumble of keys.

"They open all kinds of things," Mr. Ends answered.

"How do I know which one to try?"

"If it were me," said Mr. Ends, "I would choose the one that seems the most lonely."

Sofia nodded, but she didn't really understand what he meant. How could a key be lonely? It was just a piece of metal. Still, she looked closely at the keys in the box, and to her surprise, there *was* one that seemed to stand out from the others. Even more peculiar, there was nothing particularly interesting about it. It was definitely old, the kind of key Sofia knew was called a skeleton key, with a circular handle, a long shaft, and a tip featuring two toothlike points. Other than that, it was hardly worth noticing. Still, she picked it up.

"This one," she said.

The man shut the box. "Ah," he said. "You've selected a whichkey."

"Witch key?" said Sofia. "Like, it belonged to a witch?"

Mr. Ends shook his head. "*Which*," he said. "Because you can never be sure *which* thing it will open."

Sofia laughed. "Well, I hope it opens the trunk in our attic," she said.

"Do you?" asked Mr. Ends.

Sofia nodded. "Sure," she said. "I want to see what's in there."

The man looked at her, another smile playing at the corners of his mouth. "In that case," he said, "I have a feeling you'll find that this key is exactly what you're looking for."

When Sofia and her dad got home, she ran up the stairs to the attic. Inside, she knelt on the floor in front of the trunk. She took out the whichkey and gripped it in her hand. She slipped it into the lock on the trunk, then held her breath as she turned it.

There was a click. Sofia put her hands on either side of the lid and lifted. This time, it opened.

2

Sofia peered into the trunk.

The only thing she saw inside was a stuffed teddy bear. She lifted it out and examined it. It was very old, but it looked well loved, with several mended tears and a button sewn on where one of its eyes had fallen out.

"You were obviously somebody's favorite," Sofia said as she set the bear on the floor and examined the trunk more thoroughly. Using the flashlight she'd brought with her, she shined the light inside, allowing her to see more clearly. The sides were lined with paper covered in a pattern of faded pink roses. Then she noticed something on one side, toward the bottom: a small tear in the paper. One corner curled up. Curious, Sophia tugged at it, and it pulled away even more.

Sofia poked her fingers into the opening she'd made. She felt something. Tugging on it, she pulled out a small envelope. It wasn't sealed, and it contained a piece of paper. She slipped it out and opened it. Inside were two coins. Sofia had never seen anything like them. On one side was a woman's head surrounded by stars. On the other was a V, which Sofia knew was the Roman numeral 5. Based on that, she guessed that maybe the coins were nickels.

She slipped them into a pocket of her jeans and looked at the paper. There was writing on it.

Happy 10th birthday to my darling son.

I hope you are feeling better. I'm sorry we cannot be together. But we will see one another soon and have a real celebration with cake and ice cream and presents.

Your loving mother

"My darling son," Sofia said. She looked down at the teddy bear. "Is he the one you belong to? I wonder what his name was."

She turned the envelope over, looking for a name written on it, but there was nothing. Sofia returned the note to the envelope and placed it back behind the trunk's paper lining. She looked for more hidden secrets, but found nothing. Then she noticed that inside the top of the trunk someone had written the letters *JBW* in pencil. In several places, the paper was stained with dark patches. Sofia ran her fingers over the lid, and felt a prickle run down her arms. There was something disturbing about it.

She put the teddy bear back inside the trunk and shut the lid. Now she really wondered what the attic had been used for. At ten years old, the boy who presumably owned the trunk would have been too young to be renting a room from someone. And he had apparently been sick. Had he been sent there to stay with relatives, or maybe friends of his family? And what had happened to him?

Just then, the door to the attic banged shut

behind Sofia, making her jump. She spun around, shining the flashlight. "Papa?" she said. "That's not funny!"

There was nobody there. Just the closed door. At first, Sofia thought a breeze must have blown it shut. *But there's no open window here*, she reminded herself. Suddenly feeling a little scared, she walked quickly to the door and turned the handle. To her relief, the door opened easily. She opened and shut it a couple of times, reassuring herself that she wasn't locked in, then closed it so that it couldn't bang closed and startle her again. As she pressed her hand against the wood, her fingers felt a series of scratches there. She shined her flashlight on the area and discovered that the back of the door was covered in little groupings of six vertical marks, with a seventh one running horizontally through them.

Weeks, Sofia thought. *They indicate weeks. Seven days for each one.*

She counted the marks. There were twelve groups of them, plus one additional group with only three upright scratches. If they really did indicate weeks, that added up to about three months. Sofia stared at the door. Had someone—the boy whose things were in the trunk, maybe—really stayed in the attic for that long?

The room was dark and dreary. It would have been hot in the summer and probably cold in the winter. Suddenly, Sofia didn't want to be in there anymore.

She yanked the door open and shut it behind her. Then she went downstairs to the kitchen, relieved to be in a room filled with light and air. Her father was seated at the table, eating a sandwich. "Hey, there," he said. "I was just about to call you for lunch. Did the key work?"

Sofia nodded as she sat down and picked a potato chip off the plate in front of her.

"That's great!" her father said. "Any treasures inside the trunk?"

"No," Sofia said. "Well, maybe these." She fished the two coins from her pocket and held them out.

"Those are Liberty Head nickels," her father said. "My grandfather had one in his collection."

"Are they valuable?"

Her father shook his head. "Not very," he said. "Although those look like they're in mint condition, so they're probably worth a little bit. We can look them up online later. You found them in the trunk?"

Sofia nodded. She hesitated, then said, "Do you think anything bad happened here?"

"Bad?" her father said. "Like what?"

"I don't know," Sofia said. "Like, maybe someone died?"

"Old houses have a lot of history," her father said. "I suppose someone might have died here. But if anything really bad happened, I think the Jackstraws would have told us about it."

"Maybe they didn't know," Sofia suggested.

Her father set his sandwich down. "Did something scare you up there?" he asked.

"No," Sofia said quickly. "I was just wondering, is all."

"We could probably do some research on the house's history," her father said. "That might actually be fun. Maybe we could find some old photos of it and hang them up. I bet guests would like that."

"Sure," Sofia agreed. But her thoughts were on the trunk in the attic, and the boy it might have belonged to. She wanted to know more about *him*.

"I'll add that to the to-do list," her father said, sighing. "Right after repairing the roof, painting the rooms, fixing the plumbing . . ." He leaned back in his chair. "I'm going to need another sandwich if we're going to get all this work done."

They finished lunch, then spent the afternoon taking down the old wallpaper in one of the bedrooms. Sofia found pulling the strips of paper off strangely satisfying and soon forgot all about the attic and what she'd found there. By the time they'd finished the room and had dinner, she was so tired that she happily went to bed, where she returned to reading *The Children of Green Knowe.* The story was about a boy who comes to stay in a house where three ghost children also live. Sofia was curious to see how it ended, but she was so tired that she fell asleep with only five pages left.

She woke up when she heard a bang, followed by the sound of footsteps overhead. At first, she thought it must be an animal, maybe a rat or a squirrel that had gotten in. But then the sound came again, and she realized that the steps were far too heavy to be those of something so small.

Someone was walking around in the attic.

Assuming it was her father, she closed her eyes and tried to go back to sleep. But then the sound came again. When she opened her eyes, she looked at the clock on her bedside table and saw that it was 3:33 in the morning. Why would her father be walking around in the attic so late?

He wouldn't, Sofia told herself.

Now she was wide awake. And she had a choice to make. She could either lie there in bed and be frightened thinking about what might be making the noise in the attic, or she could go find out what it was. That might make her even *more* scared, but the truth was probably way less scary than anything she could imagine in her head.

Before she could talk herself out of it, she got out of bed, picked up the flashlight sitting on the bedside table, and left the room. Going to the attic stairs, she shined the light up at the door. It was still closed.

Sofia crept up the stairs, trying not to make

a sound. When she reached the top, she pressed her ear to the door, listening. She thought she might hear someone moving around, but there was nothing. She waited for what seemed like forever, and still no sound came from behind the closed door.

Just as she was about to turn around and head back to bed, Sofia heard a scratching sound coming from the other side of the door. She gasped, and the sound stopped. Then she heard the distinct sound of footsteps moving away from the door.

Her heart pounding, Sofia put her hand on the doorknob. But for some reason, she couldn't bring herself to turn it. "Who's there?" she called out.

There was no answer.

Sofia opened the door. She shined the

flashlight all around, but there was no one in the attic.

Maybe it really was just a squirrel, she thought. She looked at the worn areas in the roof. It was possible that a squirrel could get inside. A squirrel jumping from the beams to the floor might make noises like footsteps. And a squirrel scratching at the door to get out also made sense.

That's what it was, she told herself. *A squirrel.*

For a moment, she felt relieved. Then she decided to look at the back of the door. If a squirrel had been scratching at it, there should be some marks. And there was one. But instead of random scratches, it was a new mark on the last row of days. Where before there had been three upright lines carved into the door, now there were four.

3

The Sorrow's Hollow library was small. Very small. In fact, it was really just one room with nine rows of shelves and a big wooden desk where the librarian sat. There wasn't a computer to be seen, or cheery signs announcing a summer reading program, or anyone browsing the new titles—all three of them—displayed on a small table near the entrance.

"I don't think anyone is here," Sofia said as she and her father looked around.

"Shh!" hissed someone unseen.

"Must be the resident ghost," Sofia's father joked.

"I assure you, young man, I am not a ghost," said a firm but soft voice. An elderly woman materialized from between two rows of shelves. Not even as tall as Sofia was, the woman had long gray hair that was neatly braided in a single thick rope that hung down her back. She had sharp features, gleaming dark eyes, and a firm-set mouth. She was dressed in faded blue overalls and a red flannel shirt, even though it was summer and hot as anything. But she seemed cool as could be as she regarded Sofia and her father with a curious but not unfriendly expression. "You're new," she said.

"Henry Flores," said Sofia's father. "And my daughter, Sofia."

"Jackson Quinn," the woman said. "But everyone calls me Jack, so you might as well do that too."

"Are you the librarian?" Sofia asked.

"I am," Jack said. "As much as anyone is, anyway."

"What do you mean?" Sofia asked.

"Town doesn't really have a librarian," Jack explained. "Nor a library, come to mention it." She nodded at the shelves. "This is my personal collection. Well, part of it. I change the books out every week or so depending on how many have been checked out and whether or not the cows are calving."

"Cows?" Sofia said.

"I run a dairy farm," Jack explained. "The

library is kind of a side job. Not that I get paid for it. So, what brings you to Sorrow's Hollow?"

"We're opening up a bed-and-breakfast," Sofia's father explained.

"You don't say," Jack remarked.

To Sofia, it sounded like the librarian didn't think this was the greatest idea. "We bought the old Jackstraw house," Sofia informed her.

One of Jack's eyebrows lifted, but only for a moment. "Heard somebody had," she said. "Interesting house, the Jackstraw place."

"That's why we're here," Sofia said. "We were hoping you could tell us more about it."

"That I certainly can," said Jack. "What would you like to know?"

"Everything," Sofia blurted.

"Well, I don't think I know *everything* about it," Jack said. "But I know a lot. Before the

Jackstraws—those would be the people you bought it from, of course—it was owned by the Children's Wellness Society."

"What's that?" asked Sofia.

"A charity founded in the middle of the nineteenth century," Jack explained. "They built your house in 1877, I believe. Used it to house children who came down with various diseases."

"You mean a sanatorium?" Sofia said.

Jack nodded. "I see somebody reads a lot of books," she remarked. "Indeed, it was a sanatorium. It wasn't called the Jackstraw house then, of course, on account of the Jackstraws hadn't bought it yet. Back then it was called Fever House."

Fever House. Something about the name sent a shiver of fear through Sofia's body. It sounded like a place from a nightmare. "Why?" she asked.

"Because the children sent there were all afflicted with scarlet fever," Jack said. "It swept through the area starting in 1890. Killed a whole lot of people. The hospitals were full, so people who couldn't find beds there ended up in places like Fever House. Especially children whose parents and other relations were sick too."

"That explains all the beds," Sofia said to herself. "In the attic," she added when she saw Jack looking at her. "There are fourteen of them up there."

"Still?" Jack said. "I'm surprised. Anyway, the Society disbanded when there was no more use for them, and the Jackstraws bought the place in 1955. They raised seven kids there."

"Do you know anything about any of the kids who stayed at Fever House?" Sofia asked. "Are there records anywhere?"

"No records that I know of," Jack said. "The Society members kept to themselves, mostly. And townsfolk didn't like going near the place if they didn't have to. On account of the sickness."

"That makes sense," Sofia's father said. He put his hand on Sofia's shoulder. "Well, you solved a big part of your mystery, *mija*."

Sofia nodded. "Thank you," she said to Jack. "This is a good start."

"You're very welcome," Jack said. "Now, is there anything else I can do for you today? If not, I've got to get home to milk some cows."

"That's it for now," said Sofia as she and her father walked to the door.

"You might also want to talk to Edward Jackstraw," Jack said. "He's the only Jackstraw still living in the Hollow. He teaches English at the high school, but in the summer he and Gus run an ice cream stand out by the lake. Can't miss it. It's the only one there. He might know more about the house, seeing as how he grew up in it."

"Good idea," Sofia said. "I'll go see him tomorrow."

"You'll have to wait a few days," Jack told her. "He's visiting his parents at their new place in Florida. Be back Friday, I think."

"We can drive out there then," Sofia's father told her. "Sound good?"

"Sure," said Sofia. "Thanks again," she added to Jack.

Sofia and her father left the library and

walked down the main street, back to where they'd parked the truck by the little grocery store.

"Sounds like our house has an interesting history," Sofia's father said as they went into the grocery store and got a cart.

"Yeah," Sofia agreed. She was thinking about the attic again, and about the kids who might have lived in there. "Is scarlet fever really dangerous?" she asked her father as he searched through a bin of onions, looking for a perfect one.

"It can be," he said. "And it certainly was back in the day, before they knew how to treat it." He placed the onion in the cart and looked at Sofia. "You're thinking about all those sick kids, huh?"

Sofia nodded. "It must have been really scary for them."

"I'm sure the people who ran the charity

took good care of them," her father said. "I bet they—"

"Excuse me," said a woman. "Are you Henry Flores?"

Sofia looked at the woman who had interrupted them. She was tall and thin, with pale white skin and black hair tucked into a tight bun at the base of her neck. She wore a simple white dress that made her look even more pale. Her only makeup was bright red lipstick that made her mouth look like a rose. Her eyes were a strange violet color, pretty but also a little unnerving.

"Yes," Sofia's father answered her. "I am. And you are?"

"Melissa Hoovert," the woman said. She held out a business card. "I'm an interior designer. I hear you're renovating Fever House."

Sofia found it curious that the woman didn't call the place the Jackstraw house, like everyone else did. She wasn't old, so maybe she was just interested in history.

"I thought maybe you could use some help renovating the house," the woman continued. "I've worked on many of the homes in town. I know it's a lot for one person to do, and—"

"He's not just one person," Sofia said. "I'm helping too."

Melissa Hoovert looked down at Sofia and smiled tightly. "Of course you are," she said. "All I meant was that there are a lot of decisions to make when renovating a historic home, and I'd like to offer my services."

"Thank you," Sofia's father said. "That's very kind of you."

The woman smiled and tilted her head.

For some reason, Sofia didn't like the way she was looking at her father. Sofia pulled on his sleeve. "We need to get stuff for dinner," she reminded him.

"Right," her father said, shaking his head as if he'd forgotten. He smiled at Melissa Hoovert. "Thank you for the card, Mrs. Hoovert," he said.

"Oh, there is no Mr. Hoovert," the woman said. "It's Miss Hoovert. But you can call me Melissa."

"Okay, Melissa," said Sofia's father. "Maybe you'll hear from me."

"I do hope I will," Melissa said as Sofia practically dragged her father away.

"I'm hungry," Sofia said. "Let's just get stuff for dinner and go."

Her father pushed the cart down the aisle.

Sofia, looking over her shoulder, saw Melissa Hoovert watching them as she pretended to examine the jars of tomato sauce. Then, weirdly, it seemed as if she started to shimmer. Sofia thought she could almost see the rows of jars behind her. Sofia blinked and looked again. Nothing seemed out of the ordinary. Sofia let her gaze linger for a moment too long and her eyes met Melissa's. A chill ran down Sofia's back. She quickly turned away and headed after her father. There was something very strange about that woman.

She hoped they never saw her again.

4

The next day, Sofia was once more helping her father strip wallpaper in one of the bedrooms when she heard a voice call out from downstairs.

"Hello! Henry? It's Melissa!"

Sofia turned to her father. "You called her?" she asked accusingly.

"It can't hurt to see what ideas she has for the house," her father said.

Sofia tugged a piece of wallpaper free and grunted to hide her annoyance. A moment later, Miss Hoovert walked into the room. Sofia ignored her, concentrating on the wall in front of her.

"Oh, this room is *delightful*," Melissa said. "It gets so much light. What color are you thinking of painting it?"

"We were thinking maybe blue?" Sofia's father said. "Sofia picked out a nice cornflower color."

"Hmm," Miss Hoovert said, sounding like she didn't approve. "I don't know. Blue can be so cold. What about yellow?"

"Oh, yellow would be much better," Sofia's father said. "Don't you think so, *mija*?"

"No," Sofia muttered. Why was her father listening to this woman's advice, as if he and

Sofia couldn't make decisions perfectly well on their own?

"There are nine bedrooms if I remember correctly," Melissa said. "Maybe one of the other ones could be blue."

"You've been in our house before?" Sofia asked. She knew she sounded angry, but she couldn't help it. She didn't like the way the designer was acting as if she knew what was best for *their* house.

"Oh, no," Miss Hoovert said. "Not until today. I must have seen it on the realtor's listing when it was for sale. Nine bedrooms and four bathrooms. Isn't that right?"

"Exactly right," said Sofia's father, as if Melissa had just given the correct answer to the winning question on *Make Me a Millionaire!*

"We'll look at each and every one," the designer said. "I have oodles of ideas."

Oodles? Sofia thought. *Who says oodles?*

"Henry, why don't you give me the full tour?" Melissa suggested.

Before Sofia's father could answer, a loud bang came from above them.

"What was that?" Miss Hoovert said. She looked anxiously at the ceiling.

"I don't know," Sofia's father said. "Maybe the door blew shut somehow? Or something fell over?"

"There's nothing up there," Sofia said. "Just the trunk and the cots."

Miss Hoovert gave a small gasp. Sofia looked at her. Her face was even more pale than usual. And could Sofia see the dresser Melissa was standing in front of? That was impossible. But for just a moment she swore she could look right through Melissa. She even saw the vase of flowers sitting on the dresser's top. Then it was gone.

"Is everything all right?" Sofia's father asked.

"The noise just startled me, is all," Melissa said. "I'm fine."

"I'll get you something to drink," Sofia's father said. "How does lemonade sound?"

Miss Hoovert smiled nervously. "That would be wonderful. Thank you."

Sofia's father left the room. Sofia wasn't happy about being left alone with Miss Hoovert, and tried to ignore her by focusing on pulling more wallpaper off. But the woman wanted to talk.

"You said something about a trunk," Melissa said. "Do you think that's what made the noise?"

Sofia shook her head. "I shut it," she said.

"Unless someone else opened it again, it couldn't slam closed. And it's only me and my dad in the house."

She noticed Miss Hoovert was staring at the ceiling again. "And how did you get the trunk open?" she asked.

"I found a key," Sofia answered. *But how did you know it was locked?* she thought to herself.

"A key," Melissa said. "Where did you get that?"

"I found it," Sofia lied. For some reason, she thought it was best that Melissa didn't know exactly where she'd gotten the key. "In a box of junk in the basement."

"I see," said Miss Hoovert. Then, for a second time, she uttered a little shriek of fright.

Sofia turned around. Melissa was staring at the dresser. There, next to the vase filled with daisies and black-eyed Susans that Sofia had picked from the yard, sat the teddy bear from the trunk. It leaned against the wall, its mismatched eyes seeming to stare at Miss Hoovert.

"How . . . how . . . how did that get in here?" the woman stammered.

Sofia was wondering the same thing. She had definitely put the bear back in the trunk. And she didn't remember seeing it on the dresser when she set the vase there. She would have noticed it for sure. But there it was.

Miss Hoovert turned away from the bear. "That shouldn't be here," she said, sounding angry. "You should get rid of it."

"Why?" Sofia asked. "It's just a teddy bear." Sure, it was weird that the bear was there, and Sofia wondered how it had gotten there too. But it was still only a stuffed animal.

"It will frighten guests," Melissa said. "Just get rid of it. I need to go now."

"What about your tour?" Sofia asked.

"I can see the house later," Melissa said. She glanced at the bear and appeared to shudder. "Once that *thing* has been taken care of."

She left the room. Sofia followed her. Together, they went downstairs and into the kitchen, where Sofia's father was pouring lemonade into three tall glasses.

"I was just coming back up," he said as he handed a glass to Melissa. Then he noticed her face. "Are you all right? You look like you've seen a ghost."

"I'm fine," Miss Hoovert said, although Sofia could see that her hand was shaking.

"Great," Sofia's father said. "Hey, when we're done with our lemonade, would you like to drive into town and look at paint colors at the hardware store?"

Melissa drained her glass. "I think that's a wonderful idea," she said.

"Do you mind staying here by yourself for a little while?" Sofia's father asked his daughter.

Sofia shook her head. Staying there by herself was exactly what she wanted.

When her father and Melissa got into the truck fifteen minutes later and drove away, Sofia wasted no time in returning to the bedroom, picking up the teddy bear, and going up to the attic.

The top of the trunk stood open. Sofia stared at it for a moment. Part of her was scared. Since her father had been with her in the bedroom when the noise occurred, it couldn't have been him making the sound.

Something—or someone—else was responsible for the noise. And for bringing the teddy bear down to the bedroom. But she hadn't heard or seen anyone enter the room.

She thought about Tolly, the boy in *The Children of Green Knowe* who discovered that the strange things happening in his house were caused by ghosts. This gave her an idea. "Okay," she said, pushing her fear aside and trying to sound brave. "I don't know who—or what—you are. But if you want to be friends, I'm okay with that."

She stood there in the silence, her heart beating in her chest. Then she heard a noise and looked over at the one cot that still had a mattress on it. The springs were squeaking, as if someone was sitting on it. She saw an indentation form in the mattress. She walked over to the cot and stood near it.

"Is that you?" she said. "Are you here?"

Instinctively, she held out the teddy bear. A moment later, she felt something, as if fingers brushed against her own. Then the sensation faded as the teddy bear seemed to float through the air away from her. It hovered for a moment over the cot, as if someone was hugging it. Then it settled on the mattress.

Sofia looked at the bear, then at the spot on the mattress where an invisible body would be. She sensed that the spirit was waiting for her to respond.

"I still don't know who you are," she said. "But I'm going to take that as a yes."

5

The next morning, Sofia woke up to rain. She also woke up thinking about the spirit in the attic. She'd decided to call it a spirit because *ghost* sounded too, well, dead. Not that she was afraid of ghosts (at least, she didn't think she was, although she'd never met one) or anything. *Spirit* just sounded friendlier, and the person (she didn't want to call it a thing) in the attic seemed nice. At least to her. It obviously didn't like Miss Hoovert. *Then again, who would?* Sofia thought as she got up and rummaged around in her closet for some clothes.

When she went downstairs, she found her father making pancakes. He was singing to himself as he cooked, and seemed really cheery despite the rain that spattered against the windows.

"You're in a good mood," Sofia observed.

"I had a good time with Melissa yesterday," her father said.

Outside, thunder rumbled and the rain fell harder. It almost sounded angry.

"Take a look at the paint colors she picked out," Sofia's father continued, and the sky grew darker.

Sofia glanced at the pile of color sample cards stacked neatly beside her plate. "Maybe later," she said. She wanted to ask her father what he liked about Melissa, who she found to be really awful. But she didn't want to sound like she was being peevish (this was one of her favorite words, which she'd learned from reading a lot of fantasy books by writers like E. Nesbit and Edward Eager), and so she concentrated on eating the pancakes her father plopped onto her plate a minute later.

"Melissa invited us to go out to dinner tonight," her father said, sitting down across from Sofia and talking louder to be heard over a thunder boom. Sofia couldn't help but notice the rumbling seemed to happen every time he mentioned the interior designer. "She says she knows this good Thai restaurant, and thought we could go there tonight and talk more about the house. She has some really great ideas for how we could turn this into something special."

"You already have great ideas," Sofia said, swirling a bit of pancake around in the syrup she'd poured over the stack. "Why do you need more?"

"It's always good to get other perspectives," her father said. "Besides, how lucky are we that we found an interior designer right here in Sorrow's Hollow?"

"I think the two of you should go," Sofia suggested. "I feel like having spaghetti tonight, and I want to finish reading my book."

"You're sure you don't mind being here alone?" her father asked.

Sofia shook her head. "Nope," she said. "I'll be fine." It was weird that her father was giving in so easily, and part of her was a little bit hurt that he wasn't trying harder to get her to go with him. But the whole thing with Melissa was also weird, and until she figured out why, she wasn't going to get too upset. Besides, she really did want to be alone in the house. She had something planned.

As the day wore on, the rain kept coming. Sofia was so busy doing various tasks around the house, though, that she actually kind of liked it. There was something fun about being safe and dry inside while it stormed outside.

Around five o'clock, her father came into the room where she was painting the baseboards with a fresh coat of white paint. "I'm leaving to meet Melissa," he said as a crack of lightning sizzled overhead.

"Have fun," Sofia said. "Don't stay out too late."

Her father laughed. "Okay," he said, coming over and giving her a kiss on the top of her head. "I'll see you in a few hours."

As soon as he was gone, Sofia went into action. Going to her room, she took out a word game from her closet. Then she gathered up a flashlight and several of the battery-powered candles her father had bought in case the power went out, and carried everything up to the attic. When she got there, she discovered that the plastic her father had stapled over the holes in the roof the day before had mostly worked to keep the rain out. There was only one spot he had missed. Water dripped onto the floor below, but only a little bit.

She arranged the candles on the floor. When she turned the candles on, she was surrounded by a soft glow, almost as if they were real candles. This made her feel like she was inside a warm cocoon. The rain continued to patter on the roof overhead, and thunder growled like an angry animal, but Sofia felt safe.

Opening the board from the game, she laid it on the floor in front of her. Then she took the tiles that had letters printed on them and placed them right side up around the board, leaving an open space in the center. When she was done, she looked around the room. "Okay," she said. "I don't know if this will work or not, but I'm going to try. I know you can move things around, so if you want to talk to me, move the tiles to spell words. Okay?"

She waited, staring down at the board in front of her. For a minute, nothing happened. Then one of the tiles—a *Y*—slid from its position on the left side of the board and moved to the clear spot in the middle. This was followed by an *E*, then an *S*.

"Yes," Sofia said, her heart beating excitedly. The spirit was talking to her. "Good. That's good."

She had so many questions, she didn't know what to ask next. She decided to start with, "What's your name?"

This time, the tiles moved more quickly, as if the spirit had gotten the hang of moving them and was eager to talk. *J-O-H-N*, it spelled.

"Nice to meet you, John," Sofia said. "I'm Sofia."

But the spirit wasn't done. Next, it spelled out *B-R-A-D-L-E-Y*. Then there was a pause and it started a new word. *W-A-T-S-O-N* appeared underneath the first two names.

"John Bradley Watson," Sofia said. "That's a

good name." Then she remembered the letters written inside the lid of the trunk. "JBW," she said. "So, the trunk did belong to you. How old are you, John?"

The tiles spelling out the spirit's name were swept back with the others, and a new word formed: *E-L-E-V-E-N.*

"A year older than me," Sofia said. "We could be in the same grade in school, though, because I skipped ahead." She hesitated, not knowing how to phrase her next question. It was a big one. "Are you . . . a ghost?" she asked.

Y-E-S, John wrote.

Although Sofia had pretty much known this must be the answer, she still felt sad. "How did you become a ghost?"

Outside, a huge crack of lightning split the sky. Sofia jumped. The rain intensified, beating angrily on the roof. On the board, the tiles began to swirl around, faster and faster. The letters became a blur, then flew off the board in all directions, scattering across the attic floor. Then a wind swept through the attic. Weirdly, the battery-powered candles went out as if they were the real kind, leaving Sofia in the dark. She reached for her flashlight and clicked it on, but it didn't work. She tried the button several times, but it was as if something had drained the batteries. She was sitting in pitch-blackness.

"John?" she said. "Did you do that?"

There was no answer.

"John?" she tried again. "It's okay. We're friends, remember? I want to help you."

Again, the only response was the sound of the storm howling around the house.

"Okay," Sofia said. "I guess you're not ready. I'll try again. But could you make my flashlight work, please? I don't want to fall down the stairs."

She waited. A few seconds later, her flashlight came on.

"Thanks," Sofia said. She collected the candles, then started to gather the tiles that were strewn around the attic. When she had them all back in the box, she put the cover on and picked the game up. "I'll talk to you later, John," she said. "And I'm sorry about what happened to you."

She left the attic, closing and locking the door. Back in her bedroom, she put the game away, then went downstairs to make herself some spaghetti. As she waited for the water to boil, she thought about what had happened in the attic. *I talked to a ghost*, she thought. *That's totally weird.* And yet, it didn't *feel* weird. If anything, it had felt like talking to a friend. "A friend who just happens to be a ghost," she said aloud.

As she ate her dinner, she thought about what she should do next. She had a lot of questions. And she thought she knew where to start getting some answers. Tomorrow, she was going to pay a visit to Edward Jackstraw.

6

On Friday, Sofia's father announced that since the rain had stopped and it was now bright and sunny, he and Melissa were going to go on a picnic. This time, he didn't even invite Sofia to come with them. He'd been acting strangely ever since coming home from their dinner date the night before. He wouldn't stop talking about how wonderful the designer was, and how every single idea she had for the house—from the chandeliers she recommended for the foyer to the types of flowers she suggested they plant along the front walk—was the most amazing, clever thing anyone had ever thought of. Sofia was totally sick of hearing the name Melissa Hoovert, and she was relieved that her father was going to be out for the afternoon so that she wouldn't have to hear about the woman for a little while.

Exactly *why* her father was so into Melissa and her thoughts about the house was something Sofia had to set aside while she focused on the bigger mystery—how John Bradley Watson had died. And to try to find answers about that, she needed to start with the only person she knew of who might have any information about the Jackstraw house's past, someone who had lived there.

Riding her bike out to the lake was easy enough. The road there was flat, and it wasn't terribly hot. All the same, by the time Sofia arrived at the Frosty Freeze, she was tired, and a root beer float sounded like just the thing to make her feel better. She parked her bike and walked up to the window where customers placed their orders. There she was greeted by a man with twinkling blue eyes and silver hair buzzed into a flattop. "Welcome to the Frosty Freeze," he said warmly. "What can I get you?"

"Are you Edward Jackstraw?" Sofia asked.

"I'm Gus," the man answered. Then he turned and called out, "Eddie! There's a young lady here to see you." Then he turned back to Sofia. "He's not in any trouble, now, is he?" he asked, pretending to sound serious.

"Well, he *might* be a suspect in a break-in,"

Sofia said. "I'm going to need to ask him a few questions."

"Who is it?" a man asked, appearing from the back of the shop and wiping his hands on a dish towel.

"I didn't get her name yet," Gus said. "But I hear you've been on a crime spree. Is that what you're doing on those nights you tell me you're playing poker with the boys?"

Edward Jackstraw peered out the window at Sofia. Like Gus, he had silver hair, but his was a little longer. Also, he wore glasses, and his eyes were brown. "You look a little young to be a detective," he said.

"My name is Sofia Flores," Sofia told him. "I live in your old house. Jack at the library told me you might be able to tell me a little bit about it."

"Well, I might be able to," Edward said. "How about I come out there and we sit and talk at one of the picnic tables? What are you having?"

"A root beer float, please," Sofia said.

"Coming right up," Gus said. "You two go talk. I'll bring it out to you."

Sofia walked over to one of the picnic tables placed in the grass behind the Frosty Freeze. A moment later, Edward Jackstraw came and sat across from her. "Mom and Pop mentioned that some nice people bought the place," he said. "How are you liking it?"

"It's good," Sofia said. "Mostly."

"Mostly?" Edward said. "Is there something wrong?"

Sofia wasn't sure how to answer him. "Jack said the house used to be a sanatorium," she said. "For sick kids."

Edward nodded. "That's right."

"Do you know if any of those kids died?" Sofia asked.

Edward sighed. "Scarlet fever was pretty serious. Some of them did. There's actually a section of the Sorrow's Hollow cemetery for them."

Sofia hesitated. "Do you know if any of them died from . . . other things?" she asked.

"Other things?" said Edward. "Like what?"

"Like, maybe, murder?" Sofia said just as Gus arrived with her float.

"Murder?" Gus said, setting the float down. "You said he was just a burglar. Is there something else I should know?"

"Get back to work," Edward teased. "If your boss sees you goofing off like this, he'll fire you."

"Oh, yeah?" Gus said. "If he fires me, then my boss isn't getting the meat loaf he likes so much for dinner tonight." He looked at Sofia. "If he gives you any trouble, you call me. I used to be a police officer, and I still have some moves."

Sofia laughed as Gus walked away. She liked Gus and Edward, almost as much as she disliked Melissa.

"So, what's this about?" Edward said as Sofia stirred the ice cream in her float.

Now that she'd started the conversation, Sofia wasn't sure how to proceed. She wanted to tell Edward everything, but it sounded so ridiculous. "Did you ever experience anything unusual while you lived in the house?" she asked instead.

"Unusual how?" said Edward, looking at her with interest.

"Like, um, in the attic?" Sofia said. "Noises? Things moving around on their own?"

For a moment, Edward looked nervous. "So," he said, "you met the ghost."

Sofia set her spoon down. "You know about John Bradley Watson?"

"You named him?"

"I didn't name him," Sofia explained. "That's just his name."

"How do you know that?" Edward asked.

"He, um, told me," said Sofia. "Last night."

Edward looked surprised. "He *talked* to you?"

Sofia shook her head. Then she explained what she had done with the tiles. When she was finished, Edward laughed. "That's very clever," he said. "I wish I'd thought of doing that."

"But you believe me?" Sofia said. "About there being a spirit?"

"I do," Edward said. "When I was a boy, I often heard someone moving around in the attic. But none of my brothers and sisters did, and they all said I was making it up."

"You weren't," Sofia assured him. "He's there."

"I never actually went into the attic," Edward told her. "I was too afraid. You're really brave to have done it."

Sofia shrugged. "Thanks," she said coolly, but inside she was really pleased about being called brave. "I asked John how he became a ghost," Sofia continued. "He wouldn't answer me. I think if he died from scarlet fever he probably wouldn't be upset about saying so."

She sipped her root beer float, enjoying the

creamy sweetness of it while she waited for Edward to say something. The man was looking at her with a strange expression, part sad and part afraid. Sofia wondered if she had said something wrong. "Is everything okay?" she asked.

"I just hadn't thought about her in a long time," Edward said.

"Her?" said Sofia.

"The woman in white," Edward said. "That's what I called her. I used to dream about her a lot. I don't know who she was, really. A nurse of some kind, maybe. But the dream was always the same. I was in a bed in the attic, sick, and she would come in with a tray of food. A bowl of soup and some bread. But I knew that the soup was poisoned, and that I shouldn't eat it. She would always bring it to me and try to give it to me. I would start yelling, then wake up in my own bed. It happened almost every night for about a year."

"Then what?" Sofia asked.

"The dreams just stopped," said Edward. "Right around my twelfth birthday."

"John said he was eleven," Sofia said. "Maybe when you turned twelve, your connection to him stopped."

Edward Jackstraw looked at her. "You're a very interesting girl," he said.

"I like to think about things," Sofia said. "I wonder if you were dreaming about what happened to John. Like, maybe he was trying to show you."

"Maybe," said Edward. "All I know is, I was really glad when the dreams stopped. Then I forgot all about them. Until now."

"I'm sorry," Sofia said. "I didn't mean to make you remember something bad."

"It's all right," Edward said. "I'm glad you did. And I'll try to help you figure out what happened to John Bradley Watson."

"You will?" Sofia said. "How?"

"My mother collected a lot of material about Sorrow's Hollow over the years. She always wanted to write a book about the town, but never got around to it. When she and my father moved, she left her collection with me. I'll look through it and see what I can find. Do you have a cell phone? I can text you if I find anything."

"I do," Sofia said. She recited her phone number as Edward entered it into his own phone. "And thanks for believing me. Not a lot of people would."

"I might not have if it wasn't for those

dreams," Edward admitted. "They were so real. If I was experiencing what John did, I want to help figure out what happened to him."

Sofia drank the last of her float. "Me too," she said. "But right now I have to get back home. Dad and Melissa will be back soon."

"Is Melissa your mother?" Edward asked.

"Oh, no," said Sofia. "She's the interior designer who's helping him with the house. Melissa Hoovert. You probably know her since Sorrow's Hollow isn't that big."

"I don't," Edward said.

"That's weird," said Sofia. "She said she's worked on a lot of the houses in town. Anyway, they'll be getting back soon, and I should be there when they do. How much do I owe you for the float?"

"Nothing," Edward said. "It's on the house."

“Thank you!” Sofia said. “That’s really nice of you.”

“Consider it a thank-you for telling me the most interesting story I’ve heard in a long time,” Edward said.

“It sure is interesting,” Sofia agreed as she stood up. “I just hope it has a happy ending.”

7

"Engaged?"

Sofia stared at her father, sure she had misheard him. Melissa was standing next to him, and he had his arm around her waist. The woman was smiling at Sofia, but her violet eyes sparkled triumphantly, as if she had won a contest.

"Isn't it wonderful, *mija*?" Sofia's father said. "We're going to be a happy family."

"Yes," Melissa purred. "Very happy. I've always wanted a daughter."

"I am *not* your daughter," Sofia said angrily. "And you are definitely *not* my mother."

She turned and ran from the room, her father calling out for her to come back. She ignored him, stomping up the stairs to her bedroom and slamming the door. Flinging herself onto her bed, she lay staring up at the ceiling, her mood growing darker and darker. As if responding to her, the sky outside the windows grew darker too, the fluffy white clouds that dotted the blue expanse like sheep suddenly turning into snarling black wolves. A low grumble of thunder rolled overhead, and once again the rain came.

Someone rapped on her door. "*Mija*?"

"I'm sleeping!" Sofia answered.

The door opened. "Then you must be talking in your sleep," her father said. "Can I come in?"

Sofia turned onto her side, not answering. Her father walked over and sat down on the bed. He put his hand on her shoulder. Sofia shrugged it off. "I know this is a surprise," he said. "It's a surprise to me too."

Sofia grunted but didn't say anything.

"I know once you get to know Melissa, you'll love her as much as I do."

I will not, Sofia thought.

"She wants to get to know you," her father continued. "If you'd just give her a chance, I know you'll—"

Sofia rolled over. "There's something wrong with her," she said. "She says she's from Sorrow's Hollow, but I think she's lying."

"Lying?" her father said, his voice sharp. "Why would she lie about that?"

"I don't know," said Sofia. "But Edward says he's never heard of her, and—" She stopped, realizing that she'd said too much.

"Who's Edward?" her father asked.

"Nobody," Sofia muttered. "I'm just saying, you shouldn't believe everything she says."

Her father stood up. "I know you're upset about this, but I'm disappointed in you for making up stories about Melissa. I think you owe her—and me—an apology."

"What?" Sofia said. Her father was looking at her with an angry expression. "You're mad at *me*? She's the one you should be worried about. She—"

"Enough," her father said. "I don't know what's gotten into you, but I don't like it. I think you should stay up here and think about what you're going to say when you come downstairs again."

He left the room, shutting the door with an angry bang. Sofia stared at the door, tears welling up in her eyes. Her father had never spoken to her like that. He was always kind, even when they had disagreements.

"She's done something to him," she said. "I know it."

She didn't know what to do next. She was absolutely not going downstairs where her father and Melissa were. But she also didn't want to just sit in her room being angry. She decided to go to the attic and see if she could get John to talk to her.

Taking the word game and bag of candles with her, she left her room. As she passed the landing, she heard the sound of Melissa laughing, and the angry knot in her chest tightened. She hurried along, climbing the stairs to the attic.

As she had before, she arranged the candles on the floor and turned them on. Then she spread the tiles out on the board and took a deep breath. "Hi, John," she said. "I know you got upset last time. I'm sorry. I didn't mean to make you remember anything bad. Can we try again?"

Almost immediately, the tiles spelled out *Y-E-S*.

Sofia breathed a sigh of relief. "Great," she said. "I made a friend who wants to help too. His name is Edward Jackstraw. He used to live in this house. Do you remember him?"

N-O, the tiles answered.

"I guess maybe you never actually saw him," Sofia said. "He said he never came up here. But he heard you sometimes. And he wants to help figure out if you were—what happened to you."

She hesitated, afraid that she would make John disappear again. "Are you okay talking about that?"

There was a long pause, and Sofia started to think the spirit had gone quiet again. But at least he hadn't thrown the tiles around. Since they still spelled out *Y-E-S*, she decided that John was agreeing to talk.

"You had scarlet fever, right?" Sofia continued. "And that's why you were here."

Again, the letters didn't move. Sofia took a deep breath. "But that's not how you died, is it?"

Now the letters did move, the *Y*, *E*, and *S* sliding apart as the *N* and the *O* took their place.

"I didn't think so," Sofia said. The air grew chilly. Sofia shuddered and rubbed her bare arms. She was about to ask another question when the tiles moved, spelling out *O-L-I-V-E*.

"Olive," Sofia said, not understanding. "Is that a person?"

M-O-S-S-H-E-A-R-T appeared on the board in answer. Then a deafening peal of thunder shook the house. Sofia heard lightning slice across the sky. Wind howled around the house, shaking it. The flames of the candles flickered but didn't go out, and the air around Sofia crackled with electricity.

"It's okay," Sofia said. "I know this is hard to talk about." Then she remembered something.

"Edward told me he used to dream about a woman," she said. "Someone who was trying to poison him. Is that what happened to you?"

Three new tiles spelled out *Y-E-S* beneath the name of Olive Mossheart. The tingling feeling in the air intensified, and Sofia's hair lifted up and floated out around her. The energy was incredibly strong, as if revealing his deepest secret was empowering John's spirit.

Suddenly, the air in front of her began to shimmer. A form took shape, and moments later, a boy was standing in front of Sofia. Not a solid, human boy but the image of one. Sofia could see the attic walls through his body. He was about her age, wearing overalls and a T-shirt. He had light-colored hair and was shoeless. He stared at Sofia with dark eyes.

"Hi, John," Sofia said. "It's nice to meet you."

The spirit boy nodded but didn't speak. Sofia wondered if he could. Then John turned his head, looking at the door behind him.

"You made those marks, didn't you?" Sofia asked.

John nodded.

"Because of Olive Mossheart," said Sofia. "The woman Edward dreamed about. She poisoned you."

Again, the spirit nodded. He turned back to Sofia, and his expression was angry.

John nodded slowly. Thunder boomed overhead.

"Were you the only one?"

John shook his head.

"But why?" Sofia said.

John shook his head again.

"You don't know," said Sofia. "Okay. We'll try to figure that out. At least we have a name now."

A knock on the door interrupted the moment. "Sofia?" her father called. "What are you doing in there? Are you all right? The storm knocked the power out."

The door handle rattled as he tried to get in. Then another voice spoke. "Tell her to open it. Now."

John's spirit body glowed brighter. His eyes widened. Sofia gasped as the electric feeling around her intensified. On the board, the tiles spelling out *O-L-I-V-E M-O-S-S-H-E-A-R-T* began to rearrange themselves.

M-E-L-I-S-S-A, they spelled out, then *H-O-O-V-E-R-T.*

Sofia stared at the board. She looked up at John. There was more banging on the door.

Sofia felt like she might be sick. "Olive Mossheart and Melissa Hoovert," she said. "They're the same person."

8

I have information.

Sofia looked at the text message from Edward Jackstraw. She was in her room, lying on her bed. Actually, she was *locked* in her room. She'd discovered this when she'd woken up and tried to get out, only to find the door somehow secured from the other side.

The previous night had been horrible. Her father hadn't believed her explanation that she'd been in the attic because she'd heard a noise. Even though she'd tried to hide the candles and board game beneath John's cot, Melissa Hoovert had seen them, and convinced Sofia's father that Sofia was up to something. He'd ordered Sofia to apologize for being rude earlier, and when she'd refused, he'd told her to go to her room. With the power out, she hadn't even been able to read. All she could do was lie on her bed and be angry.

Eventually, she'd fallen asleep. That's when someone had locked her in.

Can you meet me at the Frosty Freeze?

Sofia started to text back that she couldn't. Then she had an idea. Yes, she wrote. Be there in half an hour.

She slipped her phone into her pocket, put her sneakers on, and went to the window. Her bedroom happened to be located just above the house's front porch. She slid the window up, and climbed out and onto the porch roof. She paused there when she heard voices coming from below.

"How long should I keep her in there?" her father said.

"Until she learns her lesson," Miss Hoovert replied. "You've been far too lenient with her."

Hearing the woman's voice, Sofia felt herself get angry as she thought back to the previous night. She didn't know how it was possible that Olive Mossheart was alive now, but she was convinced it was true.

"I still don't know what she was doing up in the attic," Sofia's father said.

"Causing trouble," Melissa said. "Keeping her in her room where she can't get into any mischief is the best thing for everyone."

"She must be getting hungry by now," said Sofia's father.

"Don't worry," Melissa Hoovert said. "I'll make her some soup later. My own special recipe."

Sofia resisted the urge to shout down to her father to get away from the horrible woman. But she knew he was under some kind of spell and wouldn't listen, no matter what Sofia said. She was going to have to figure out another way to get rid of Melissa. First, she had to get off the porch roof without being seen.

Fortunately, the porch wrapped around the side of the house. Sofia carefully crept along the wall until she was around the corner. Then she went to the end, where there was a trellis extending up from the porch railing. It was covered in morning glories, and Sofia was screened from view as she climbed down. When she reached the porch, she jumped to the ground. Then she darted around the side of the house to where her bike was still parked beside the kitchen door.

She pedaled harder than she ever had in her life, anxious both to be away from Melissa Hoovert and to find out what information Edward Jackstraw had found. When she arrived at the Frosty Freeze, she was panting and sweaty.

"Looks like you could use a root beer float," Gus said when he saw her. "I'll tell Edward you're here."

Sofia sat down at a picnic table, happy to be in the shade. A minute later, Edward appeared carrying a glass in one hand and a manila folder in the other. He handed the drink to Sofia, then sat down across from her. "I found some things in my mother's collection that I think you'll find interesting."

He opened the folder and took out a piece of paper. "This is an article from the *Sorrow's Hollow Wailer*, the newspaper of the time."

"'Twelve souls departed this world in one fell swoop as the Angel of Death passed over Fever House on Tuesday last,'" Sofia read. "Wow. They couldn't just say that twelve people died?"

"I guess not," Edward said. He held out something else. "There's this too. It's a photograph of the woman in charge of running Fever House. Her name was—"

"Olive Mossheart," Sofia said, staring at the picture. "I know. It's also a photo of Melissa Hoovert."

"The woman you told me about?" said Edward. "That's impossible. This photo is over 125 years old. It must be someone who looks like her."

"It's her," Sofia said. "Their names are anagrams." She plucked a pencil from Edward's shirt pocket and scribbled on the paper. "See?"

"I want to say that's a coincidence too," Edward said. "But something tells me it isn't. And there's more. This is also the woman from my dreams when I was eleven."

"Really?" Sofia said.

"I must have seen a photo of her somewhere," Edward said. "Maybe my mother left it out and I caught a glimpse of it."

Sofia sighed. "I don't think so. I think you were seeing what John saw." She looked at Edward, who looked more than a little upset.

"I don't think those kids died of scarlet fever. I think it was her."

"What makes you think that?" asked Edward.

"John told me," Sofia said. "Last night. She gave them her soup, just like in your dreams. And now I think she's come back as Melissa Hoovert."

"That's—"

"Crazy?" Sofia said. "I know. The worst of it is, I think it's my fault."

"Yours?" said Edward. "How could it be your fault?"

"I opened the trunk," Sofia explained. "And the next day, she showed up. I don't think it's a coincidence." She reached into her pocket and took out the key. "The man who sold me this said something strange. He said that keys can open all kinds of things. I thought he meant all kinds of ordinary doors, or trunks, or whatever. Now I wonder if he meant doors to the past. I think maybe when I opened the trunk I somehow opened a door to that time, and Olive Mossheart came through. Only now she calls herself Melissa Hoovert. And she wants Fever House back."

"But what would a trunk have to do with anything?" Edward asked.

"I don't know," Sofia said. "Yet."

Edward Jackstraw tapped the photo of Olive Mossheart with his finger. "You're sure that's the same woman?"

"Positive," Sofia said. "That's why John got so agitated when he heard her voice in the house, and why it storms every time she's around or someone mentions her. And now she's tricked my dad into thinking he's in love with her." Sofia stood up. "I have to go," she said.

"What are you going to do?" Edward asked.

Sofia stared hard at the photograph lying on the table. "Stop Olive Mossheart, Melissa Hoovert, or whatever her name is from hurting anyone else."

9

“There you are,” Melissa Hoovert said when Sofia walked in the door. She was standing at the stove, stirring a big pot with a wooden spoon. She tapped the spoon on the side of the pot, then turned to look at Sofia. Her violet eyes glimmered wickedly. “That was very naughty of you, sneaking off like that. Your father and I were very worried. Weren’t we, Henry?”

Sofia looked at her father, who was seated at

the table. His eyes had a glassy look to them, as if he was under some kind of spell. He frowned. "Yes, darling," he said. "Very worried."

"We'll discuss your punishment later," Melissa said. "Right now, it's time for lunch. Why don't you sit down? I've made some of my famous vegetable soup."

"I'm not hungry," Sofia said defiantly.

"Don't be rude, Sofia," her father said. "Melissa has gone to a lot of trouble to make soup for us. Sit down and have some."

"I don't want anything she's made," Sofia said.

Miss Hoovert, ignoring her, ladled some soup into a bowl. Carrying it to the table, she set it down in front of Sofia's father. "Here you are, dear," she said.

"Don't eat it!" Sofia said. "It's dangerous!"

Melissa laughed. "Dangerous?" she said. "Whatever gave you such a wild idea?"

"I know who you are!" Sofia said. "And I know you poisoned all those kids when you lived here before."

"Lived here?" said Miss Hoovert. "Me? Sofia, I think maybe you're coming down with something. You're talking nonsense. Do you have a *fever*?" She spoke the last word with emphasis, looking directly into Sofia's eyes.

Sofia's father picked up a spoon and dipped it into the soup. He lifted it to his mouth.

"No!" Sofia said, dashing over to him and knocking the spoon from his hand. Soup splattered on the floor.

"Sofia!" her father exclaimed. "What's gotten into you?"

Melissa walked over, a rag in her hand. She

knelt and wiped the spilled soup from the floor. She picked up the fallen spoon and took it to the sink. Then she got a clean spoon and returned to the table. Putting it into the soup, she raised it to her lips and daintily sipped it, watching Sofia the whole time. When she was done, she said, "Delicious."

"Says you," Sofia scoffed.

"Would I eat my own soup if I'd done something to it?" Melissa asked.

"You're already dead," said Sofia. "Well, you're something. I don't know what. I bet poison wouldn't hurt you."

"Already dead?" Melissa said. She laughed. "Did you hear that, Henry? Now she's accusing me of being a zombie." She stuck her hands out in front of her and moved them around jerkily. "Argh," she said, rolling her eyes up into her head. “Grr.” She laughed. “Sofia, I don’t know *what* has gotten into you.”

“I think you should go to your room, young lady,” her father said, sounding angry. “I’ll be up later to have a talk with you.”

“Fine,” Sofia said. “But don’t eat any more of that soup.”

She stomped up the stairs to her room and slammed the door. She had no intention of staying there and waiting to see what Melissa Hoovert had in mind for her, but she needed time to think. She couldn’t just call the police and tell them that a woman who had lived more than a hundred years ago was trying to poison her. And she didn’t know how to get rid of Melissa herself.

She sat on her bed, thinking. As she did, she absentmindedly put her hands in her pockets.

There she found the whichkey and the nickels she'd taken from the trunk in the corner of the attic. Rubbing them between her fingers, she got an idea.

She opened her door, making sure nobody was outside waiting for her. She heard the murmuring of voices downstairs, and hoped Miss Hoovert and her father would keep talking long enough for her to do what she needed to do.

She raced to the attic, went inside, and locked the latch. She found her way to the little window and rubbed it as clean as she could with the sleeve of her shirt. Enough light came through it that she could see well enough to go to John's bed and pick up his teddy bear. She took it with her to the center of the room, where she sat down and held it in her lap. Then she placed a nickel in each hand and closed her fingers around them.

"John," she said, trying to keep her voice quiet. "I need your help. Olive Mossheart wants to hurt me like she hurt you, and I don't know how to stop her."

The air in front of her began to shine. A moment later, the spirit of John Bradley Watson stood before her. Sofia opened her palms. "These belong to you," she said. "Your mother sent them to you. Take them."

Ghostly fingers reached out. When they touched the coins in Sofia's hands, the coins began to glow, and Sofia felt them become warm. The glow expanded, filling the insubstantial form of the spirit boy with golden light. It traveled up his wrists and into his arms, then kept going. Soon, it filled John's whole body, as if touching something that had come from his world helped him become whole again. After a minute, Sofia was looking at what appeared to be a very real boy.

"Thank you," John said aloud.

"You can talk!" Sofia said happily.

John picked the coins from her palms and held them up. "My mother sent me these," he said. "For my birthday."

"Yes," said Sofia. "I took the letter out of your trunk. I'm sorry."

"It's all right," John told her. "I hid them in there so nobody would steal them. I'm glad you found them."

"We don't have much time," Sofia said. "She's going to come looking for me."

John's face clouded over with anger. "She poisoned us," he said.

Sofia asked a question she had been thinking about. "How come you're the only one here?

In the attic, I mean. Where are the others?"

John looked sad. "Someone had to stay and make sure she didn't get out."

"Get out?" Sofia said. "Out of where? The attic?"

John pointed at the trunk. "Out of there," he said. "She was a ghost even back then. I don't know how, or why. She was just here. But I did trap her in the trunk." His expression grew angry. "I shut her in there," he continued. "She opened my trunk to take my things out of it. I was able to push her inside and lock it. And when I became a ghost, I stayed. To make sure she didn't escape and hurt anyone else."

Sofia was deeply saddened by John's story. He'd been waiting for more than 125 years for his mother to come for him. Sofia knew what it felt like to lose a mother, to wish she would come back, just once, to hold you and tell you she loved you. The thought of waiting for more than a century for that was unbearable. Then another terrible thought occurred to her.

"But I let her out," she said. "With the whichkey. It's all my fault." She looked at John. "I'm so sorry."

"You didn't mean to," he said. "She was waiting, all this time. It's what she's wanted more than anything. That key did more than just open the trunk. It opened a door that let her come back."

"The key didn't just unlock the trunk," Sofia said. "It unlocked the past. It brought her back. We have to find a way to stop her."

"The key," John said. "If it let her out, maybe it can send her back again."

Sofia thought about this. "You mean, if we can get her into the trunk and lock it?"

John nodded.

"Sofia!" Melissa Hoovert's voice came from outside the attic. A moment later, the sound of a fist banging on the door exploded into the room. "Open this door! It's time for your soup, young lady."

John looked at Sofia. "There's no time," he said. "We have to do it now."

"What do I do?" Sofia asked.

John pointed at the door. "Let her in."

10

With a trembling hand, Sofia unlatched the attic door and pulled it open.

"It's time for your soup," Melissa Hoovert said.

Sofia backed away from the woman. Melissa came closer. As she entered the attic, something strange happened. She began to change. Her modern dress faded, transforming into the dress she had been wearing in the photograph Edward Jackstraw had shown Sofia. By the time she was halfway across the attic floor, she looked exactly as she had on the day John Bradley Watson locked her inside the trunk. She was once again Olive Mossheart. John himself was standing in the shadows, hidden from view. But Sofia could sense him waiting.

Olive didn't seem to notice the change in her appearance. She held out the bowl of soup toward Sofia. "Go on," she said. "Eat it before it gets cold."

"I don't think so," Sofia said.

Olive sighed. "This is becoming tiresome," she said. "Just eat the soup."

"She said she doesn't want any."

Hearing John's voice, Miss Mossheart started. The bowl in her hands fell to the floor, shattering. "You!" she hissed as John emerged from the shadows.

"I'm not afraid of you anymore," John said as he walked toward her.

Olive drew herself up and pointed a finger at him. "Stop!" she commanded.

"You can do nothing to me," John said. He ran at her, his hands stretched out.

Miss Mossheart growled as John crashed into her. She grabbed at his hair, trying to wrestle him away. He kicked at her as she clawed and spat. "Sofia!" John shouted. "The trunk!"

Sofia ran to the trunk. She threw the lid up. "It's ready!" she called out.

John pushed Olive Mossheart toward the trunk. Seeing it, the woman struggled. "No!" she wailed. "I won't go back!"

John shoved her. She stumbled as her legs

hit the side of the trunk. She fell backward, landing inside. Sofia slammed the trunk shut and jammed the whichkey into the lock. She turned it, pulled the whichkey out, and stepped back. The attic was deathly quiet.

"Is she . . . gone?" Sofia asked.

"I think the key finally sent her back to wherever she came from," John said.

Sofia breathed a sigh of relief. "What about you?" she asked John. "Can you leave now?"

John smiled. "I think I could," he said. "But I don't know if I want to. This is kind of my home now."

Suddenly, Sofia remembered something. "My father!" she said.

She raced downstairs to the kitchen. There, she found her father still seated at the table. He was looking around, confused, as if he'd just woken up. Sofia ran over to him and hugged him.

"What happened, *mija*?" he said. "Did I fall asleep here? I don't remember coming into the kitchen. In fact, I don't remember much at all. Have I been sick?"

"You had a fever," Sofia said. She kissed him on the cheek. "But you're better now."

Her father looked down at the bowl on the table. "Did you make me soup?" he asked.

"You don't want to eat that," Sofia said, quickly picking up the bowl and taking it to the sink, where she dumped it out. "It's cold. I'll make you some new soup."

She opened a can of chicken noodle soup and heated it up. As her father ate it, Sofia sat across from him, her thoughts lingering on the attic. Had she really sent Olive Mossheart back to her own time? And what would become of John now? He'd existed as a spirit in the house for more than a century. Would he be gone now?

That night, she lay in her bed, listening for signs that someone—or something—was still in the attic. But no sounds came from above her head, no footsteps or voices. Eventually, she fell asleep and started to dream. In her dream, she was standing in front of the attic door. She turned the knob and the door swung open.

The attic was empty. The cots that had lined each side were gone. John's trunk and teddy bear were gone. There was nothing there but dust. For a moment, Sofia felt sad. Despite saying that this was his home, John had apparently left. But then the air began to glow, and John appeared in front of her. He smiled. "Hi," he said.

"Are you okay?" Sofia asked.

Behind John, another form appeared. Sofia felt her heart begin to race. "John!" she cried. "Watch out!"

But John just smiled again. "It's all right," he said as a woman materialized. But it wasn't Olive Mossheart. This woman had a kind face. She put her hands on John's shoulders.

"Sofia, this is my mother," John said.

John's mother looked at Sofia and smiled. "Thank you," she said. "For bringing us together again."

Sofia didn't know what to say. She thought she might start to cry, she was so happy for John and his mother. Then John held out his hand. "I want you to have this," he said.

Sofia looked at the nickel resting on his palm. She reached out and took it.

"To remember me by," John said.

"I don't think I could ever forget you," Sofia told him, closing her fingers around the coin. "And I have something for you." She reached into her pocket and took out the whichkey. "Here," she said, handing it to John. "Maybe, wherever you go, it will unlock a door and let you come back to visit me someday."

John took the key and put it in his pocket. Then he and his mother faded away, their light dimming until the attic was once again dark.

Sofia woke up. She wasn't in the attic; she was in her own room. Outside her window, the moon was full and bright. She felt happy. The dream had been a good one, not scary or sad at all.

She realized that she was holding something in her hand. Opening her fingers, she saw the nickel from her dream resting there. Had John really given it to her? Or had she kept one of the nickels from earlier? She thought she'd given them both to John, but maybe she hadn't. Or maybe she'd made up the whole thing in the first place.

She decided it didn't matter. However it had come to be there, the nickel would always be a reminder of her encounter with John Bradley Watson. She would keep it forever. She closed her fingers around it again, feeling it press into her palm. *Tomorrow,* she thought, *she would ride her bike to the Frosty Freeze and tell Edward Jackstraw what had happened.* Maybe together they could find enough evidence to tell the true story of the children of Fever House and what had happened to them.

ANOTHER SCARE, IF YOU DARE!

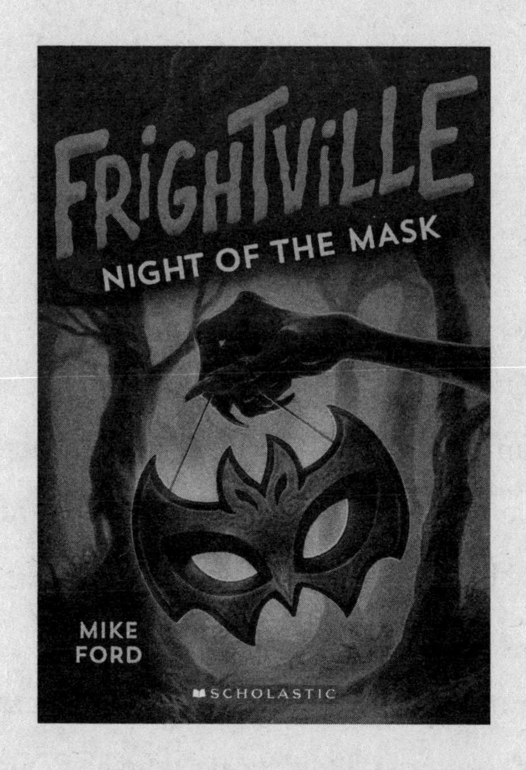

TURN THE PAGE FOR A SPOOKY SNEAK PEEK!

1

Tucker opened the small gold envelope that had his name written across the front in perfectly printed letters, and removed the pink card from inside. Instead of having ordinary writing on it, it was engraved like a fancy invitation.

COME CELEBRATE SASHA'S BIRTHDAY! it said.

"It's Saturday," said Sasha, who just moments ago had handed Tucker the envelope and was still standing in front of him, smiling widely.

Before Tucker could even read the rest of the card, she continued. "It starts at two o'clock. You don't *have* to bring a present, but I won't be mad if you do. Oh, and it's a costume party. Well, sort of. Everyone is going to wear masks. I thought that would be fun."

"What kind of masks?" Tucker asked.

"Any kind," said Sasha. "Superheroes. Animals. Monsters. Whatever you want. And don't worry about being able to get around in your chair. The hallways are super wide, there are ramps to the doors, and there's even an elevator that goes between floors. You'll have no problem."

She darted off. Tucker looked at the invitation again, thinking about what kind of mask he might want to wear. There were so many possibilities.